# This Book Belongs To:

_____

## Date & Grade:

_____

To Arianna

#73

# SECONDANDSEVEN
### FOUNDATION

The 2nd & 7 Foundation is a non-profit organization based in Columbus, Ohio. Our goal is to Tackle Illiteracy by giving free books to 2nd graders in elementary schools all across the country. By partnering with local high school, collegiate and professional athletes we are also able to provide children with positive role models that read to them and discuss the important life lessons included in our books. This outreach also inspires athletes in the community to give back.

We would like to thank everyone who gives their time and talent to The 2nd & 7 Foundation each year:

- The Hog Mollies Writing Crew (Amy Hoying, Leah Miller, Jason Tharp)
- The Ohio State University Department of Athletics
- Participating Elementary School Teachers & Principals
- Satellite Program Ambassadors
- Board of Directors
- Current and Former Student-Athlete Readers
- FUNdamental Football Camp Participants and Volunteers
- 8-Ball Shootout Participants and Volunteers
- 2nd & 7 Interns
- Major Sponsors: White Castle, Key Bank, Roosters & Giant Eagle
- Countless Individual Donors

Thank you for sharing our passion for literacy and we hope you enjoy our 6th book!

Luke Fickell

Ryan Miller
Co-founders, The 2nd & 7 Foundation

Mike Vrabel

Cover and Interior Illustrations © 2013 Jason Tharp
The Hog Mollies & The Great Golden Gizmo. Copyright © 2013 by The 2nd and 7 Foundation

ISBN 978-1-4652-2243-5
ISBN 978-1-4652-2244-2

Printed in the United States of America

Production Date: 04/15/13
Batch numbers: 43224301, 43224401
Printed by: Walsworth, Marceline, MO ; United States of America

10 9 8 7 6 5 4 3 2 1    17 16 15 14 13

The 2nd & 7 Foundation

7949 N. High Street, Suite A

Columbus, OH 43235

www.secondandseven.com

info@secondandseven.com

# OUR MISSION

The mission of The 2nd & 7 Foundation is to promote literacy by providing free books and positive role models to kids in need while encouraging young athletes of the community to pay it forward.

# The Hog Mollies
## and the
# Great Golden Gizmo

Written by: The 2nd & 7 Foundation
Illustrated by: Jason Tharp

**Kendall Hunt**
publishing company
4050 Westmark Drive • P O Box 1840 • Dubuque IA 52004-1840

It was time for the all-school assembly, and Ruby was running late.

She scurried down the hall and noticed the custodian, Mr. Hayes, had tipped his cart. His supplies scattered everywhere!

Ruby had to climb over the huge mess to make it to the gym. She felt bad about not helping him clean up the clutter, but she didn't want to be late for the big announcement.

"Good morning boys and girls," Principal Frank said "This year our school motto is 'Kindness Is Contagious.' Does anyone know what that means?"

"This month's project will give you the chance to find out. As you leave today, be sure to grab your very own Great Golden Gizmo. We want you to use this camera to catch people being kind. Your teachers and I can't wait to see what you find!"

The Hog Mollies -- Duke, Sprout, Harley and Hoppy -- knew the importance of being kind, but they weren't sure about the 'contagious' part. "I thought only colds were contagious," Duke said. "Well, hopefully these Great Golden Gizmos will help us learn more about spreading kindness," Harley added.

While Ruby and her friend Scarlet
grabbed their Gizmos, Ruby muttered,
"Ugh, where do we begin?
How do you catch people being kind?"
"I'm not sure," Scarlet answered,
"but I guess that's what we'll learn."

"Oh, the picture is blurry and off-center," Ruby noticed. "Yeah, but look in the background!" Scarlet exclaimed. "Sprout is washing the blackboard for Mrs. Shelley. I think we just caught someone being kind."

Mrs. Shelley was so touched by Sprout's nice gesture that she was inspired to do something kind, too.

Since she knew oranges were one of her students' favorite snacks, she decided to surprise them with a special treat.

When Duke found the oranges, it made his day. He didn't know who left them there, but it made him feel special.

While walking home from school, Duke was in such a good mood from his surprise snack, he picked up every piece of litter he found along the way.

Grumpy Gus spotted Duke from his store window and was grateful to see someone helping to keep the neighborhood clean.

On his way home that evening, Gus stopped to help Harley, who was struggling with a flat tire on his bike.

Harley pedaled home singing a happy tune. It felt great to have someone help him out.

When he passed the market, he saw Grandma coming out with her hands full of groceries. He decided to stop and give her a helping hand

Grandma was thankful for Harley's good deed. Later, when the Hog Mollies met with friends at their clubhouse, they found Grandma's specialty -- a homemade pickle pie -- waiting for them.

The Hog Mollies polished off the pie and headed to the park. "Look! Mr. Hayes and his son are here," said Hoppy. "And I think their kite is stuck!"

The Hog Mollies teamed up and knew just what to do.

"Thank you for being so kind, Hog Mollies!" Mr. Hayes said

Before Ruby knew it, the month was over and it was time to turn in her project. She tried her best to capture many acts of kindness with her Great Golden Gizmo, but she still didn't understand what the school motto meant.

As she rushed down the hall with her photos, Ruby stumbled and the pictures scattered all over the floor.
"Oh no!" she cried

Ruby couldn't hold back her tears.
She bent down to pick up the photos
and noticed Mr. Hayes by her side.
"Don't cry," he said, "I'll help you."

"Thanks Mr. Hayes," Ruby replied,
"but I still don't know how kindness is
contagious and I'm about to give my
presentation to the class."

"Well, let's take a look," said Mr. Hayes, comforting Ruby. "I think the answer is in your photos. Each person that shared an act of kindness actually inspired someone else to be kind. So, spreading kindness became contagious. See . . . you got it!"

Everything finally made sense to Ruby. As she began her presentation, she smiled, grateful that she caught the kindness of Mr. Hayes . . . and eager to pass it on.

# KINDNESS CHALLENGE

Find ways to spread kindness in your life.
A group of kids helped provide these ideas:

1. Say 'hello' to someone new at school.

2. Open the door for someone.

3. Share a toy.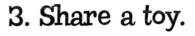

4. Help with the dishes.

5. Stand up for someone

being picked on.

# I can spread kindness by...

_____

_____

_____

_____

_____

_____

_____

_____

_____